THREE LADIES BESIDE THE SEA

RHODA LEVINE

DRAWINGS BY EDWARD GOREY

The New York Review Children's Collection
New York

THIS IS A NEW YORK REVIEW BOOK
PUBLISHED BY THE NEW YORK REVIEW OF BOOKS
435 Hudson Street, New York, NY 10014
www.nyrb.com

Library of Congress Cataloging-in-Publication Data

Levine, Rhoda.
Three ladies beside the sea / by Rhoda Levine ; drawings by
Edward Gorey.
p. cm. ,— (New York Review Books children's collection)
Summary: Two elegant ladies who live by the sea try to convince
a third to stop climbing up a tree and staring into the distance.
ISBN 978-1-59017-354-1 (alk. paper)
[1. Stories in rhyme. 2. Eccentrics and eccentricities—Fiction.] I.
Gorey, Edward, 1925–2000, ill. II. Title.
PZ8.3.L5495Th 2010
[E]—dc22
2009049192

ISBN 978-1-59017-354-1

Cover design by Louise Fili Ltd.
Printed in the United States on acid-free paper.
1 3 5 7 9 10 8 6 4 2

for Emma Walton, in her first year,
for her parents Julie and Tony,
and for Sandy Wilson

Once there were three houses
That stood beside the sea;
In each house lived a lady
Of great nobility.

There was laughing Edith of Ecstasy:
Edith so happy and gay.
There was smiling Catherine of Compromise:
She smiled her life away.

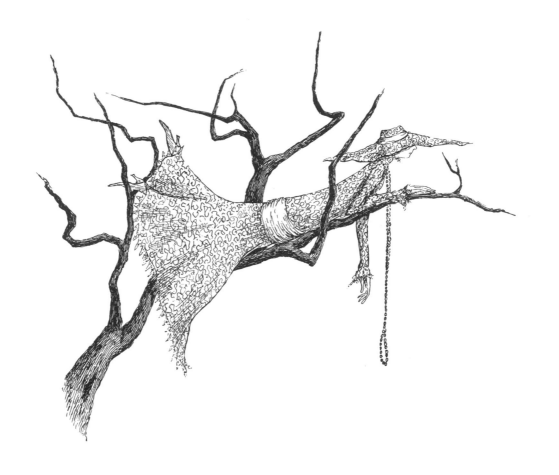

Then, there was Alice of Hazard,
A dangerous life led she:
When not indoors, involved with chores,
Alice was up a tree!

By day, these ladies kept house,
But often while stitching or cooking,
Edith and Catherine would gaze out to find
Alice—up a tree—looking!

Both Edith and Catherine kept silent
Concerning this strange, lofty feat.
Mere mention of Alice—out on a limb—
Would be, they both felt, indiscreet.

Now music was much in these three ladies' lives:
Edith plucked at a lute;
Catherine bowed an old cello string;
And, fiercely, Alice played flute.

Thursday evenings, down by the shore,
These ladies gathered together;
They played chamber works at a mad musicale,
Depending on suitable weather.

At midnight when all were played out,
Off Alice would go to brew tea;
While Catherine and Edith politely would chat
And watch the moon light up the sea.

Sometimes when left quite alone,
Edith and Catherine would question
The reason why Alice might take to a tree;
Each had a different suggestion.

Guessed Edith, "It may be she dislikes the ground,
Though that seems too strange to be true!"
Said Catherine, "Though Alice may feel quite held down,
Climbing trees is an odd thing to do!"

One Thursday night they were chatting
While Alice was off at her task.
Said Edith, "To puzzle is foolish,
About this tree matter—let's ask."

On this moonlit night Alice heard them,
And said as she poured out her brew,
"You're troubled at finding me up in a tree—
To speak the truth, I'm troubled, too.

"To tell the truth it is not easy
Not to have feet on the ground;
It's hard to sit perched on the branches
Especially on those thin and round.

"It's hard to hold on when the wind blows.
The sun, though it's warm, strains the eyes.
I love the blue sky, but I'm damp when it rains.
And, often, I'm troubled by flies.

"But, alas, I am driven up into that tree,
To search and to scan the wide sky.
I am looking out there for a bird I saw once,
Who sang to me as he flew by."

"A beauty he was, so fine and so wild
That I leapt up to herald his worth,
And only the sound of his singing
Can bring me, once more, down to earth."

"Oh, Alice," said Edith of Ecstasy,
"How silly to be in a stew.
We own birds in cages who sing pretty songs,
Pray let us lend them to you."

Then Catherine of Compromise added her voice,
"A caged bird is better than none.
You can sit by the shore with two birds at your side,
Compared to a search, that's more fun."

Alice considered their offer.
It seemed to be wonderfully sound.
How good it would be to give up that tree.
And place her two feet on the ground.

So next morning, just before sunrise,
When whitecaps rode high on the tide,
From their houses came Edith and Catherine,
Each carried a bird at her side.

Both the birds and the ladies were chirping.
They were singing a bright ancient round.
When they knocked on her door, Alice joined them in song.
They made quite a glorious sound.

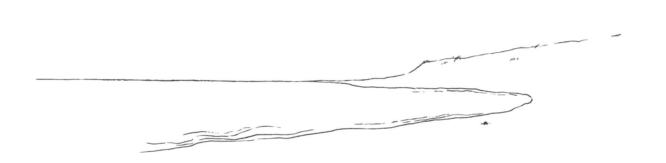

Then, at the moment of sunrise,
When the round reached a suitable end,
Edith and Catherine gave Alice the birds,
Hoping to please their strange friend.

The next days passed by very quickly.
Alice deserted her tree.
She stayed in her house and never looked out,
(Though Wednesday she walked by the sea.)

Both Edith and Catherine were pleased with their scheme;
It seemed to be working so well.
Alice was brought down to earth once again,
As surely as either could tell.

On Thursday, however, it happened!
While dusting and checking the larder,
Edith and Catherine gazed out to find,
Alice—aloft—looking Harder!

The two kindly ladies were startled;
They cried out in hearty despair,
"Oh, Alice, oh, what is the matter?
Why are you up in the air?"

But Alice was looking beyond them
As often she'd looked there before.
"Your birds were so lovely, their songs were so fine;
They made me miss my bird the more.

"I thank you for all of your kindness.
But I must remain in my tree
To look for the bird I saw once, long ago,
If I strive to endure, he'll find me."

Several years have passed by these fine ladies,
Their houses still stand by the sea.
Edith still laughs, Catherine still smiles.
Is Alice still up in that tree?

RHODA LEVINE is the author of seven children's books (two of which were illustrated by Edward Gorey) and is an accomplished director and choreographer. In addition to working for major opera houses in the United States and Europe, she has choreographed shows on and off Broadway, and in London's West End. Among the world premieres she has directed are *Der Kaiser von Atlantis*, by Viktor Ullmann, and *The Life and Times of Malcolm X* and *Wakonda's Dream*, both by Anthony Davis. In Cape Town she directed the South African premiere of *Porgy and Bess* in 1996, and she premiered the New York City Opera productions of Janacek's *From the House of the Dead*, Zimmermann's *Die Soldaten*, and Adamo's *Little Women*.

Levine has taught acting and improvisation at the Yale School of Drama, the Curtis Institute of Music, and Northwestern University, and is currently on the faculty of the Manhattan School of Music and the Mannes College of Music. She lives in New York, where she is the artistic director of the city's only improvisational opera company, Play It by Ear.

EDWARD GOREY (1925–2000) was born in Chicago. He studied briefly at the Art Institute of Chicago, spent three years in the army testing poison gas, and attended Harvard College, where he majored in French literature and roomed with the poet Frank O'Hara. In 1953 Gorey published *The Unstrung Harp*, the first of his many extraordinary books, which include *The Curious Sofa*, *The Haunted Tea Cosy*, and *The Epiplectic Bicycle*. In addition to illustrating his own books, Gorey provided drawings to countless books for both children and adults. Of these, New York Review Books has published *The Haunted Looking Glass*, a collection of Gothic tales that he selected and illustrated; *The War of the Worlds*, the pioneering work of science fiction by H. G. Wells; and *Men and Gods*, a retelling of ancient Greek myths by Rex Warner.